Fearless

by Tracey West

Illustrated by Heather Martinez

SCHOLASTIC INC.

New York   Toronto   London   Auckland   Sydney
Mexico City   New Delhi   Hong Kong   Buenos Aires

Stephen Hillenburg

Published by Scholastic Inc.,
90 Old Sherman Turnpike, Danbury, CT 06816.

SCHOLASTIC and associated logos are trademarks
and/or registered trademarks of Scholastic Inc.

ISBN 0-439-56270-8

First Scholastic Printing, October 2003

Chapters

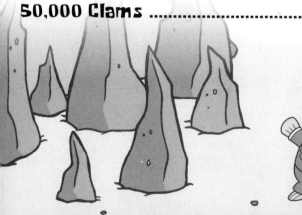

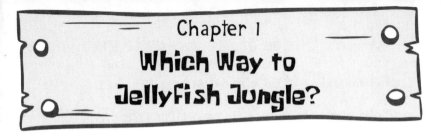

Chapter 1
Which Way to Jellyfish Jungle?

"I can hardly wait!" SpongeBob SquarePants told his best friend, Patrick. "Soon we'll be at the grand opening of Jellyfish Jungle Amusement Park. It's the jelliest place on earth!"

"Wasn't it nice of Mr. Krabs to give you the day off?" Patrick said.

"He didn't give me the day off, Patrick," SpongeBob replied. "Today is Sunday. It's my regular day off."

"No, SpongeBob," Patrick corrected. "Today is Saturday. See?" Patrick held up a poster for the grand opening of the park.

"Oh no!" SpongeBob wailed. "I'm supposed to be working at the Krusty Krab right now. We've got to go back!"

But the bus had arrived at Jellyfish Jungle.
Patrick tried to drag SpongeBob off the
bus.

"I won't go," SpongeBob said. "Turn this
bus around!"

"But it's the grand opening," Patrick said.
"We'll miss all of the jellyfish fun! I'm sure
Mr. Krabs will understand."

"Mr. Krabs *is* very understanding . . . "
SpongeBob agreed. Visions of jellyfish rides
danced in his head. It was very tempting.
"Well, we are already here," SpongeBob

finally said. "It couldn't hurt to stay just a
little while . . . "

"Hooray!" Patrick cheered.

THIS WAY TO
SUPER SCARY
TELEVISION SHOW
DON'T GO THIS WAY UNLESS
YOU ARE
FEARLESS!
JELLYFISH
JUNGLE
THIS WAY!

SpongeBob and Patrick stepped off the bus.

"Lead the way, buddy!" SpongeBob called.

"Uh, I think it's this way," Patrick said.

The two friends didn't know it, but they had made a wrong turn.

Chapter 2
Bumper Boats!

SpongeBob and Patrick had wandered onto the set of a TV show. Off in the distance, the announcer was getting things going.

"Welcome to 'Fearless,'" he said, "the show where contestants perform dangerous stunts! I'm Moe Blowfish. Our first stunt today is the Screaming Speedboat Challenge! Who will get to the finish line first?"

"Look, Patrick!" SpongeBob cried. "It's a Bumper Boats ride. Those are my favorite. And there's no line! Look out!" he shouted.

SpongeBob hopped into the nearest boat
and stepped on the gas.

Crash! Smash! SpongeBob began bumping into the other boats.

"Whee!" SpongeBob yelled. "This is just like Mrs. Puff's driving school!"

Crash! Smash! The other boats rammed into SpongeBob's boat and pushed him right across the finish line!

WHEEE

FINISH

"We have a winner!" Moe Blowfish cried.

"Contestant number 3 has zipped to first place," Moe announced. "But how will he fare in our next round—the Freaky Food Face-Off?"

"Hey, SpongeBob, who is that guy with the microphone?" Patrick wondered.

"I think he's our tour guide," SpongeBob said. "Although I have this weird feeling I've seen him somewhere before."

Meanwhile, at the Krusty Krab, Mr. Krabs turned on the TV. "Jumping jellyfish! That's SpongeBob!" Mr. Krabs cried. "He's supposed

to be working today. Why, I oughta go find that lazy loafer and teach him a lesson."

"Great idea, sir," Squidward said, without looking up from his book. "I can take care of things here."

Chapter 3
Sea-Slug Smoothies

"What should we do next, SpongeBob?"

Patrick asked.

SpongeBob sniffed. "I smell something yummy," he said. "Look! It's a snack bar. All that boat bumping has made me hungry."

"It's time to reveal our freaky food!" Moe Blowfish said, uncovering a plate of disgusting-looking food. "Sea-onion tacos washed down with sea-slug smoothies, made with fresh-squeezed sea-slug juice!"

"Sea-onion tacos? Sea-slug smoothies?
My favorites!"
SpongeBob cried.

SpongeBob ran to the table. He gobbled up every sea-onion taco on his plate. He slurped every last drop of sea-slug smoothie.

SLURP!

"Can I have more slug juice, please?"
SpongeBob asked when he was finished.

"Unbelievable!" Moe cried. "Contestant number 3 has won the Freaky Food Face-Off! That is one fearless sponge!"

"Hey, SpongeBob," Patrick said. "What do you think all these cameras are for?"

"Don't you know anything, Patrick?" SpongeBob asked. "This place is crawling with tourists. They're just making home movies."

"This tank is filled with more than 100 jellyfish," Moe announced. "We'll see which contestant can stay in the tank the longest without getting stung."

"Oh, boy!" SpongeBob said. "Swimming with jellyfish! A chance to get up close and

40

personal with the most beautiful creatures

in the sea!"

The other two contestants had to be
rescued from the jellyfish tank in seconds.

Then SpongeBob jumped into the tank.
Jellyfish swarmed around him. "I am
one with the jellyfish," SpongeBob
calmly chanted.

The jellyfish danced around SpongeBob.
They didn't sting him once!

One hour later, the announcer knocked on the jellyfish tank.

"Do I have to come out?" SpongeBob asked.

"Of course you do," the announcer replied. "You're our 'Fearless' finalist!"

"'Fearless' finalist," SpongeBob repeated. He was finally starting to understand.

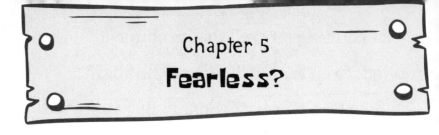

Chapter 5
Fearless?

"'Fearless'? You mean that TV show where contestants do crazy things for prizes?" SpongeBob croaked.

"Of course!" Moe Blowfish replied. "And you're our finalist. All you have to do is complete the final challenge to win the grand prize—50,000 clams!"

47

48

"But I'm not a game-show contestant," SpongeBob said.

"This *is* Jellyfish Jungle Amusement Park, right?" asked SpongeBob.

"Very funny, contestant number 3," Moe laughed. "Looks like we're ready for the final challenge. All you have to do is bungee jump over this valley of jagged rocks!"

A crane picked up SpongeBob and placed him on the cliff.

"But I'm not fearless!" SpongeBob wailed. "I'm not even supposed to be here. I'm supposed to be at the Krusty Krab!"

"You're darn right!" came a familiar voice.

SpongeBob couldn't believe his eyes. It was his boss, Mr. Krabs!

Chapter 6
50,000 Clams

"I'm sorry," SpongeBob shouted to Mr. Krabs. "I thought it was my day off."

"Get off that cliff right now, and get back to work!" Mr. Krabs yelled.

"I can't!" SpongeBob called from the top of the cliff. "I'm *AFRAAAIIIID!*"

Mr. Krabs started to climb the rocks. "If you won't come down, I'm going to come get you!" he threatened.

"What do I do?" SpongeBob thought. He could face Mr. Krabs . . . or jump off the cliff.

There was only one choice. "Here I go!" SpongeBob screamed.

SpongeBob closed his eyes . . .

took a deep breath . . .

and jumped!

"Congratulations, contestant number 3!"
Moe Blowfish cried. "You win! You *are*
Fearless!"

57

A week later, SpongeBob and Patrick were back at SpongeBob's house. "It's too bad we never got to Jellyfish Jungle," SpongeBob said.

"But you got to be on 'Fearless,' and you even won," Patrick reminded him. "Hey, what did you do with all those clams?"

"I had them sent to Mr. Krabs," SpongeBob said. "I couldn't have won if it wasn't for him."